COOL SCIENCE

SCIENCE OF Emotions

John Perritano

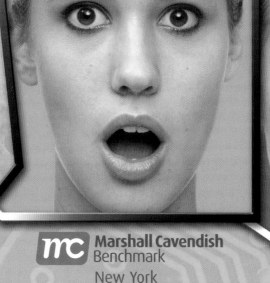

mc **Marshall Cavendish**
Benchmark

New York

This edition first published in 2011 in the United States
by Marshall Cavendish Benchmark.

Marshall Cavendish Benchmark
99 White Plains Road
Tarrytown, NY 10591
www.marshallcavendish.us

Copyright © 2011 Q2AMedia

Published by Marshall Cavendish Benchmark
An imprint of Marshall Cavendish Corporation

Other Marshall Cavendish Offices:
Marshall Cavendish International (Asia) Private Limited, 1 New Industrial Road, Singapore 536196 • Marshall Cavendish
International (Thailand) Co Ltd. 253 Asoke, 12th Flr, Sukhumvit 21 Road, Klongtoey Nua, Wattana, Bangkok 10110,
Thailand • Marshall Cavendish (Malaysia) Sdn Bhd, Times Subang, Lot 46, Subang Hi-Tech Industrial Park,
Batu Tiga, 40000 Shah Alam, Selangor Darul Ehsan, Malaysia

Marshall Cavendish is a trademark of Times Publishing Limited

Library of Congress Cataloging-in-Publication Data
Perritano, John.
The science of emotions / John Perritano.
p. cm.—(Cool science)
Includes index.
ISBN 978-1-60870-079-0
1. Emotions—Juvenile literature. I. Title.
BF531.P46 2011
152.4—dc22
2009053775

Created by Q2AMedia
Series Editor: Deborah Rogus
Art Director: Harleen Mehta
Client Service Manager: Santosh Vasudevan
Project Manager: Kumar Kunal
Line Artist: Vinay Kumar
Coloring Artists: Indrim Boo, Manoj Sharma, Nazia Zaidi
Photo research: Debabrata Sen
Designer: Rahul Dhiman

The photographs in this book are used by permission and through the courtesy of:

Cover: Yuri Arcurs/Shutterstock, Stock Photo NYC/Istockphoto, Piotr Marcinski/Shutterstock,
Christopher Futcher/Shutterstock, Jason Stitt/Shutterstock, Supri Suharjoto/Shutterstock
Half title: ZoneCreative/Istockphoto

4-5: Steve Silvas/Istockphoto; 5: Rick Diamond/WireImage/Getty Images; 6-7: Joe Brandt/Istockphoto; 8t: Yuri Arcurs/
Shutterstock; 8bl: Dns-Style Photography/Shutterstock; 8br: Zoran Karapancev/Shutterstock; 9t: Catherine Yeulet/
Istockphoto; 9bl: Cameron Whitman/Istockphoto; 9br: Photostogo; 10: Monkey Business Images/Shutterstock; 11: Avava/
Shutterstock; 12t: Gelpi/Shutterstock; 12b: Andrea Gingerich/Istockphoto; 13: Joy Brown/Shutterstock; 14: Maridav/
Shutterstock; 15: Stock Photo NYC/Istockphoto; 16: Elena Elisseeva/Big Stock Photo; 17: Kharidehal Abhirama Ashwin/
Shutterstock; 19: Chris Whitehead/Photolibrary; 21l: Joe Gough/Shutterstock; 21r: Brett Mulcahy/Shutterstock;
22: Anatomical Design/Shutterstock; 23: Aisenegger/Photolibrary; 26: Lori Carpenter/Shutterstock; 27: Anatomical Design/
Shutterstock; 28t: Tracy Whiteside/Istockphoto; 28b: Kitti/Shutterstock; 29l: George Marks/Photolibrary; 29r: Andrea Leone/
Shutterstock; 30: Amanda Rohde/Istockphoto; 31: Photostogo; 32: Muzsy/Shutterstock; 33: Imagesource/Photolibrary;
35: Nat Ulrich/Shutterstock; 36: Creatas/Photolibrary; 37: Siamionau Pavel/Shutterstock; 38: Erics/Shutterstock;
40: Arenacreative/Shutterstock; 41: Liu Jixing/Shutterstock; 42: Velychko/Shutterstock, Piotr Marcinski/Shutterstock;
43: Ifong/Shutterstock; 44-45: Lisa F. Young/Shutterstock

Q2AMedia Art Bank: 18, 20, 23, 24, 25, 34

Printed in Malaysia (T)

1 3 5 6 4 2

CONTENTS

A Roller Coaster of Emotions

You're strapped in the front car of "The Incredible Hulk," one of the most awesome roller coasters in the world. The tunnel is dark. Escape is impossible. Why did you let your friends talk you into doing this? You hate roller coasters.

Your heart beats wildly and your palms sweat as you anticipate what is going to happen next. Anticipation suddenly turns to shock as "The Incredible Hulk" rockets you 150 feet (46 meters) up through the tunnel at an ear-popping 40 miles (64 kilometers) per hour.

Shock quickly turns to fear. The coaster turns you on your head—not once, not twice, but seven upside-down, gut-twisting, you're-going-to-lose-your-lunch times.

Aaaaaaaaaaaahhhhhhhhhhhhhhhhh!

Speeding at 67 miles (108 km) per hour, you swear you will never go on another roller coaster for as long as you live. You'll never talk to your so-called friends again, either. Nope! Never!

After 2 minutes and 15 seconds of close-your-eyes terror, the ride ends. You take a deep breath. Exhilaration replaces the fear. You may even feel a bit of sadness that the ride is over. "Let's go again," your friends say. "Okay," you answer.

Anticipation, shock, fear, exhilaration, and *sadness.* These are just some of the feelings humans experience. We call these feelings emotions. Emotions often determine how we act. They affect our relationships with others. They help us sort out our thoughts and experiences. Sometimes, emotions even influence our memories.

Roller-coaster riders feel emotions ranging from terror to exhilaration.

WHAT ARE EMOTIONS?

We've all felt emotions, from happiness and excitement to sadness and fear. We also have dozens of words to describe them. But what are emotions, exactly?

Most scientists agree that emotions are a change in our mental state caused by things that happen in our lives. When we lose someone we love, we feel sorrow. When people laugh at us, we feel embarrassed. When something wonderful happens, we feel happiness. If we feel enough happiness, we can end up in a great mood!

Emotions are different from moods, though. Emotions only last for a short while. They are connected to a specific event or person. Moods last longer and are not connected to anyone or anything in particular. Instead, moods refer to overall feelings of pleasure, sadness, irritation, or **anxiety**.

Intense emotions often give rise to a physical response. People may literally "jump for joy"!

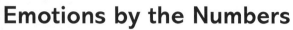

Emotions by the Numbers

How many emotions are there, exactly? Four? A dozen? One hundred? W. Gerrod Parrott, a professor of psychology at Georgetown University, has identified six basic emotions: love, joy, surprise, anger, sadness, and fear. But these main emotions, he says, branch into secondary emotions. The secondary emotions then branch into a third set, called **tertiary** emotions. Here are two examples:

	Secondary	Tertiary
Joy	Cheerfulness	Amusement, bliss, glee, delight, enjoyment, happiness, jubilation, elation, satisfaction, ecstasy, euphoria
	Zest	Enthusiasm, zeal, excitement, thrill, exhilaration
	Contentment	Satisfaction, pleasure
	Pride	Delight, triumph
	Optimism	Eagerness, hope
	Enthrallment	Bliss, rapture
	Relief	Release, liberation

Sadness	Suffering	Agony, hurt, anguish
	Sorrow	Depression, despair, hopelessness, gloom, glumness, unhappiness, grief, woe, misery, melancholy
	Disappointment	Dismay, displeasure
	Shame	Guilt, regret, remorse
	Neglect	Alienation, isolation, loneliness, rejection, homesickness, defeat, dejection, insecurity, embarrassment, humiliation, insult
	Sympathy	Pity, empathy

THE SIX BASIC EMOTIONS

Like Parrott, most researchers agree that there are at least six basic emotions. What are the six? It depends on whom you ask!

Dr. Paul Ekman, a pioneer in the study of human emotions from the University of California, San Francisco, has a slightly different list than Dr. Parrott. He states that the six main emotions are happiness, surprise, disgust, fear, anger, and sadness. Though experts disagree on the type of emotions people have, it is clear that each emotion affects us differently. Our facial expressions change. Our bodies react in certain ways. Emotions even affect how we behave.

Don't Worry, Be Happy

Happiness is a positive emotion caused by different kinds of experiences. Some people feel happy when they eat a bite of chocolate. Football fans are happy when their team wins the Super Bowl. You probably feel happy if you get a good grade, watch a funny movie, or win a contest.

Happiness is a state of mind, but it can affect our physical well-being, too.

Happiness is usually easy to spot. A happy person may smile, laugh, even jump up and down. Below the surface, happiness has other effects. It causes the blood pressure to increase, although not to the dangerous levels caused by anger. Breathing becomes more rapid. After a while, happiness can turn into the secondary emotions of satisfaction and contentment. If they happen often enough, that positive emotion and the secondary feelings that stem from it can even strengthen the immune system, which protects a person from disease.

About Face! Happiness

A happy face is pretty obvious. The corners of the mouth turn up. The cheeks bulge or rise, and the areas around the eyes crinkle. But happy expressions are also the easiest ones to fake when someone wants to hide an emotion or fool other people. Check the eyes, though. Experts say this is the area that can't easily be faked.

You can tell this person has a false smile. Although his lips are turned up, his cheeks and eyes aren't quite right.

This person has a genuine smile. The corners of her lips are raised in just the right way. The eyes crease slightly and the eyebrows dip just a little.

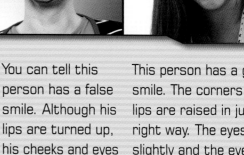

Feeling Down

Everyone feels sad at least once in a while. It's the emotion we feel when we've had a big disappointment or lost something or someone that was important to us. Loneliness and illness also trigger sadness. People can even feel sad just by seeing others who are suffering or unhappy.

Our body reacts to sadness in several ways. The most obvious way is by crying. But sadness can also cause a lack of energy and loss of appetite, both of which can lead to illness.

Sadness that goes on for too long, or becomes too painful, is called **depression**. Depression can interfere with a person's life. It can make it impossible for that person to enjoy anything, even things that normally give him or her pleasure. It's important for people who think they may be suffering from depression to get help from a doctor or psychologist.

INSIDE KNOWLEDGE

Mirror Neurons

Have you ever seen someone cry and then started crying yourself? Special brain cells called mirror neurons allow a person to feel what another person is feeling. When one person sees another person pricked by a needle or kicked in the shin, the same brain cells of both individuals become active. In other words, their neurons "mirror" one another.

Mirror neurons make us wince when a linebacker tackles a quarterback, and explain why we cry at sad movies. Scientists say mirror neurons allow us to relate to each other's feelings.

ABOUT FACE: SADNESS

The most recognizable feature of a sad expression is downturned lip corners. In addition, the eyes are narrowed, and the eyebrows are pulled together. Interestingly, sadness is also reflected in the size of the pupils. The more intense the sadness, the smaller the pupils.

Surprise! Surprise!

At some point in our lives, we are all taken by surprise. You might get a gift you didn't expect, or find ten dollars on a sidewalk. Real, spontaneous surprise only lasts for a fraction of a second before another emotion, such as delight or fear, takes over.

Surprise is a basic emotion that can be either pleasant or unpleasant. A loud noise in the middle of the night might surprise us, as will an unexpected twist at the end of a movie. When we are surprised, our jaws may drop, we might start to cry, we might even laugh. Our pulse increases and our palms sweat. The skin might become flushed.

About Face: Surprise

When a person is surprised, the upper eyelids are raised, the eyebrows go straight up, and the jaw drops. The eyebrows are actually the clearest indicator of surprise. Even when the mouth stays closed, the eyebrows go up!

That's Disgusting!

Disgust is a negative emotion. You may feel it while watching a dog gulp down something it shouldn't, or from seeing one person treat another badly.

Disgust is usually triggered by things that are dirty, offensive, or sickening. Most people become disgusted by physical things: smelling, seeing, tasting, or touching something that is revolting. We may also become disgusted by someone's bad behavior. We call this moral disgust.

We show our disgust in a variety of ways. We turn our heads, or shield our eyes from things that are physically disgusting. We may shake our head or glare at a person who has lied or misbehaved. Disgust often triggers nausea or causes people to shudder or shake.

Disgust is a powerful emotion. It can force us to turn away, but it can also attract our attention. Hollywood makes millions of dollars each year by producing horror movies that revolt us!

ABOUT FACE: DISGUST

A look of disgust usually includes a wrinkled nose with the eyebrows pulled down. The eye openings are narrowed and the lips may be pressed together. At other times, a person may show disgust by glaring at or turning away from whatever is offensive.

Scared to Death

Fear comes in many forms: fear of failure, fear of dying, fear of getting caught. You might have a fear of spiders, a fear of heights, or a fear of clowns.

Fear causes our bodies to go through many **biochemical** and physical reactions. We start perspiring. Our muscles may tighten and our heart rate might increase. Some of this is part of a fight-or-flight reaction. When we're facing a fearful situation, we can do two things: face and fight the danger, or flee. Either way, the fight-or-flight response is our body's way of dealing with fear.

The fight-or-flight response would trigger an impulse to back away from an animal like this.

Emotions in Real Life: Fear on the Hudson

On January 15, 2009, US Airways flight 1549 took off from LaGuardia Airport in New York City. Shortly afterward, several geese crashed into the plane's engines, causing the jet to lose power. Pilot Chesley "Sully" Sullenberger III guided the damaged plane to a safe crash landing in the Hudson River.

Beverly Waters was one of 150 passengers aboard the plane.

Waters said the episode was the most terrifying few minutes of her life: "Immediately, my heart started beating. It felt like it was going to beat out of my chest."

But other emotions overcame fear. As the plane floated on the river's surface, Waters said the other passengers helped each other until rescue came.

Fear is the most basic and primitive of all human emotions. It is also normal and healthy. It keeps us from harmful situations. It also helps us escape from danger.

On the other hand, some people love the "rush" that fear produces. They'll sky dive out of an airplane or climb a dangerous mountain. Moreover, many of us love to be scared when we partially know we are actually safe—watching a scary movie in a theater, for example, or going on a wild ride in an amusement park.

The body reacts to fear in a number of ways. Limbs might shake. Our body temperature may drop, and we might feel cold. We might even be "scared speechless."

About Face: Fear

It's not hard to see when someone is afraid. The eyes widen, showing the whites. The jaw drops open and the neck muscles pull tight.

Blowing Your Stack

People get angry when something doesn't go their way. The cause might be as simple as a quarter lost in a vending machine, or as major as seeing a bully beat someone up. People also get angry to different degrees. One person might become a little irritated by a situation. Another might fly off into an intense rage.

Anger causes faster breathing and tense muscles. You might clench your fists or flare your nostrils. Your eyelids may narrow, or your eyes may bulge out. Anger causes your heart rate to increase and your blood pressure to skyrocket. You might even feel like breaking something.

About Face: Anger

When a person is angry, the lower eyelids are tense and straightened. The upper eyelid is raised, and the forehead furrowed, creating a glaring expression. Eyebrows are pulled down and together. The mouth may be open, or the lips may be pressed together. Often the chin juts out.

Your Emotional Intelligence

We're lucky that emotions are easy to spot. It helps us figure out how to deal with our friends, our families—even ourselves.

Most of us are able to figure out what others are feeling by observing their facial expressions and **body language** and by listening to their tone of voice. We use this information to determine the proper reaction. How well we do this is called our **emotional intelligence**, or EI.

Let's say a friend catches you joking about him at lunch. At first, he doesn't say a word. His face turns red. He takes a step back. When he tries to talk, his voice shakes.

So what do you do? That depends on your emotional intelligence. You might apologize (good idea). On the other hand, you might tell him he's being stupid or overreacting (not such a good idea). If your emotional intelligence is really low, you might not even realize how upset he is.

People with strong emotional intelligence are able to read the moods of others and respond appropriately.

Emotional intelligence is critical to having strong relationships and friendships. It involves not only awareness of others, but also awareness of yourself. In fact, emotional intelligence is made up of several elements.

WHAT'S YOUR EI?

Emotional intelligence is...

- **self-awareness:** When you are self aware, you know your strengths and weaknesses. You know what you feel and why you feel that way. You know what your needs are and how to meet them.
- **self-management:** You manage your emotions by identifying your feelings and figuring out how to deal with them in responsible, positive ways.
- **motivation:** You use your emotions to help you achieve a goal.
- **empathy:** Through empathy, or understanding, you figure out what a person is feeling. You notice their facial expressions, their tone of voice, and other behaviors.
- **social skills:** You learn to manage your emotions and the emotions of others when you're working or playing together.

17

THE CHEMICAL CONNECTION

The causes of our emotions seem pretty obvious. When bad things happen, we feel sad. When good things happen, we feel happy. But what, exactly, makes us feel the way we do?

Part of the answer has to do with certain chemicals, called **neurotransmitters**. These chemicals carry thoughts between our brain cells, across a tiny gap called a synapse. You can think of a neurotransmitter as a sort of interpreter. It decides which feelings are connected with a thought or experience.

Some chemicals, like endorphins and norepinephrine, create feelings of extreme happiness and well-being. Serotonin can add positive feelings to an experience and relieve symptoms of depression and anxiety. (That's why it is often called the "feel good" neurotransmitter.) Melatonin relaxes us and allows us to rest.

Neurotransmitters relay, strengthen, and modify signals as they move from cell to cell.

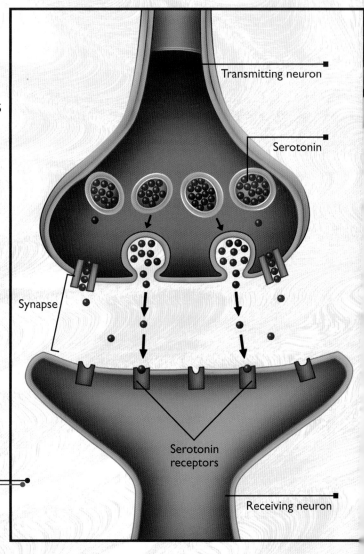

Transmitting neuron

Serotonin

Synapse

Serotonin receptors

Receiving neuron

All of these chemicals are present in our bodies. But they must be produced in the right balance, and at the right time. If they're not, a person may feel irritable or depressed. On the other hand, too much of a certain chemical might make a person feel too upbeat and **optimistic**. This can lead to bad choices and decisions.

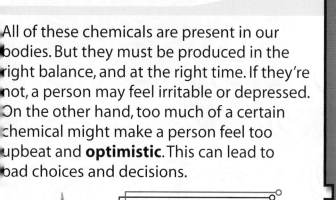
The excitement of a sports event can release a flood of chemicals—and emotions.

INSIDE KNOWLEDGE

Diet and exercise affect emotions because they affect the level of neurotransmitters. One researcher, Dr. Judith Wurtman, ran a clinical research program on serotonin at M.I.T. She believes that a diet low in **carbohydrates** ultimately leads to feelings of despair and sadness. That's because carbohydrates trigger biochemical reactions that help the brain produce serotonin. On the other hand, exercise causes the brain to release adrenaline, dopamine, and serotonin—all the feel-good chemicals. That's why many people become depressed if there's a break in their exercise routine.

EMOTIONS AND THE BRAIN

Your brain allows you to walk, talk, sleep, and eat. Your brain remembers who you are and where you live. Your brain is also the warehouse in which all your emotions are stored.

The Lovely Limbic

Inside your brain, a bundle of **nerves** is wrapped around the top of your brain stem. Those nerves are called the **limbic system**. The limbic system is where the raw materials of emotion—pleasure, pain, and memories—are mixed together. Neurotransmitters send messages throughout the limbic system.

Limbic System

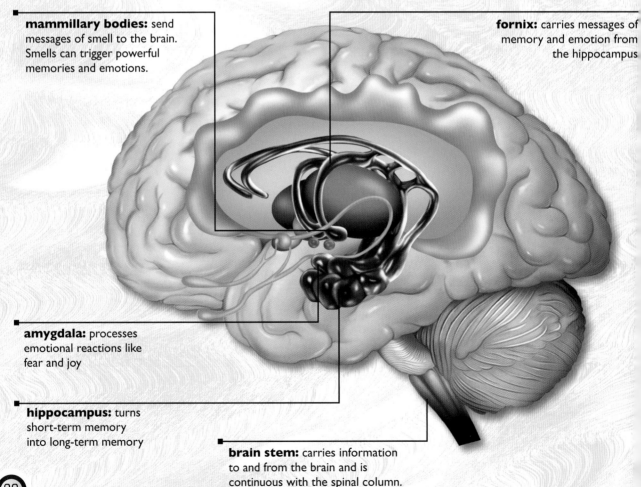

mammillary bodies: send messages of smell to the brain. Smells can trigger powerful memories and emotions.

fornix: carries messages of memory and emotion from the hippocampus

amygdala: processes emotional reactions like fear and joy

hippocampus: turns short-term memory into long-term memory

brain stem: carries information to and from the brain and is continuous with the spinal column.

When the limbic system is working the right way, our emotions are in balance. But emotions can be so intense at times that the system becomes overloaded. When that happens, a person can literally become paralyzed by fear, or left speechless.

Why is that? The limbic system is linked with other areas of the brain that deal with the heart, **respiration**, and digestion. This means intense emotions can cause high blood pressure, shortness of breath, and stomach problems. They can even cause the heart to stop beating. In other words, it really is possible to scare someone to death—so don't ever try to!

Inside Knowledge

Emotional Memory

The limbic system is part of the reason that smells, sights, sounds, and textures can trigger emotions. All of these can be part of our "emotional memories," connected in our mind with pleasant or unpleasant events. It explains why some food becomes "comfort food." It's also why some sights and sounds make people feel sad—even when they don't know why.

Memories themselves can also trigger emotions. Americans, for example, will never forget how they felt on September 11, 2001, when planes crashed into New York's twin towers. These memories and emotions stay with us throughout our lives.

Comfort foods like tuna casserole and meat loaf can actually make people feel better by triggering pleasant memories.

Brain Injuries

The frontal lobes of the brain help us control our emotions. They also help us act correctly in social situations. They stop us from doing and saying things we'd be sorry about later.

That's why a brain injury can throw a person's emotional health out of whack. People who have suffered certain types of brain injuries can be happy one moment and sad the next. They may laugh hysterically at a not-so-funny joke, or get furious if a child starts acting up at the grocery store. Sometimes they may say wildly inappropriate things.

Specific events usually trigger emotions. But those suffering from brain injuries may suddenly express their emotions without any reason, even though they never did so before. That often leaves family members and loved ones confused. They might think they have done something to set off these emotional outbursts.

Lobes of the Brain

The largest portion of the brain is divided into four lobes.

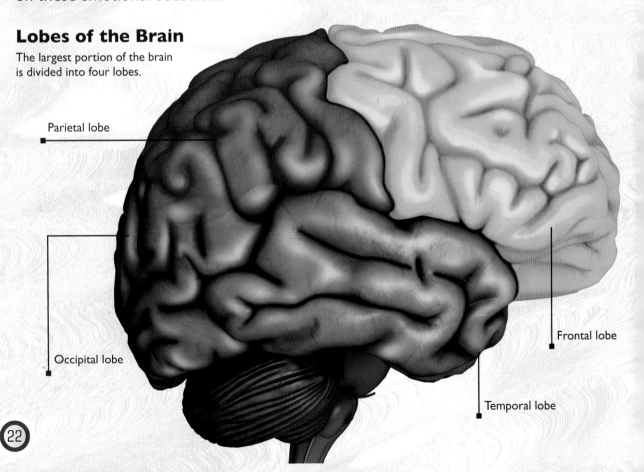

Parietal lobe

Occipital lobe

Frontal lobe

Temporal lobe

Doctors who treat brain injuries tell their patients that they should take a fifteen-minute time out to cool down when they become angry. Many times, however, brain-injured people might not even realize they are angry until it's too late. Family and friends need to force the time out, when they can—whether the person thinks it's needed or not.

Luckily, the ways we show and deal with emotions are learned behaviors. That means that even when the brain is injured, a patient can relearn those behaviors. For example, a brain-injured person can learn to stay calm by watching how others react to an upsetting event.

Another way to deal with brain injuries is through prevention. Since many accidents take place during sports or on the battlefield, steps can be taken to keep people safer. For example, helmets are now designed with hard shells and spongy insides to cushion the brain from impact.

People with brain injuries may have irrational bursts of anger. Friends and family need to help them calm down.

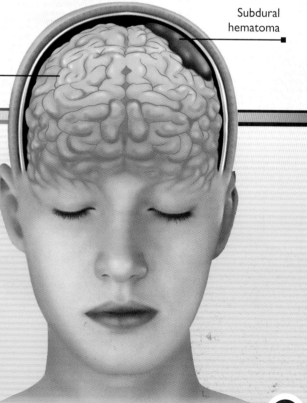

Subdural hematoma

Brain

Inside Knowledge

Subdural Hematoma

If you've ever watched a medical show, you've probably heard one of the doctors say, "It's an acute subdural hematoma. Get him to the ER. Stat!" But what is a subdural hematoma, exactly? In simple terms, it's a collection of blood on the surface of the brain. It's usually the result of a serious head injury. If the blood is not released, the brain may be permanently injured. The patient might even die.

THEORIES ON EMOTION

The brain and the body. It's clear that both are equally important when it comes to emotions. But which gets involved when?

Over the years, psychologists have developed many theories to help people understand emotions. Theories are educated guesses. By understanding how emotions work, scientists hope they can better help people manage them.

Body Before Brain

One theory about emotions was developed in the 1880s by American psychologist William James and Danish psychologist Carl Lange. Although they did their research separately, they arrived at the same conclusion, later called the James-Lange theory. Both believed that emotions start in the body, not the brain. They said humans feel emotions because they sense physical changes in their bodies.

Let's say you see a bear. James and Lange would say that your nervous system is the first to react. Your heart races, your blood pressure skyrockets, and your palms sweat. You automatically begin running away. Only then would your brain realize what's going on and make you feel afraid. Critics of this theory disagree. They say that people know they are afraid long before their body reacts.

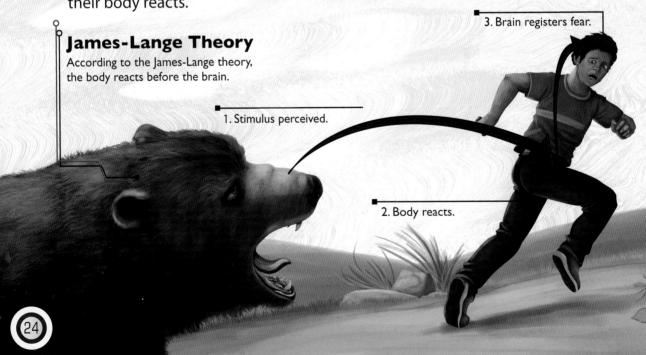

James-Lange Theory
According to the James-Lange theory, the body reacts before the brain.

3. Brain registers fear.

1. Stimulus perceived.

2. Body reacts.

Brain Before Body

James Cannon and Philip Bard were two researchers who didn't agree with the James-Lange theory. They developed their own theory. It states that emotions begin in the brain, not the body. This means that when you see that bear walking through the woods, a part of your brain called the thalamus immediately receives a message.

Inside the thalamus, the message is then split. One part goes to the brain's **cortex**, which creates fear. The other half goes to the **hypothalamus**, which tells our heart to beat faster and our muscles to tense. The brain then tells the rest of the body to run as fast as it can! Today, more people believe Cannon and Bard's theory is the correct one.

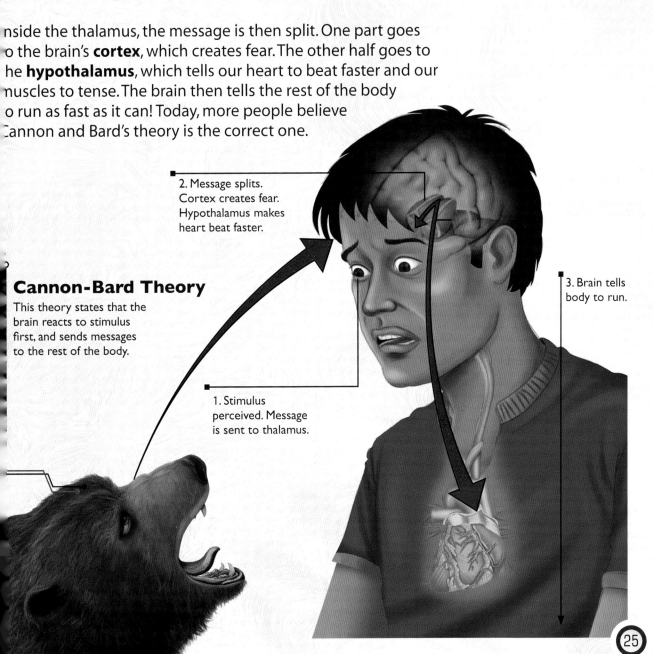

2. Message splits. Cortex creates fear. Hypothalamus makes heart beat faster.

Cannon-Bard Theory

This theory states that the brain reacts to stimulus first, and sends messages to the rest of the body.

1. Stimulus perceived. Message is sent to thalamus.

3. Brain tells body to run.

LOGIC AND EMOTION

We all like to think we make good choices and act sensibly. But emotions can influence our actions and how we deal with various situations.

Scientists believe that emotions and logic are present in every mental activity. Let's say you're deciding what to wear one morning. You think about the weather—a logical thought. But emotions are affecting your choice, too. If you're feeling worried about a test, you might choose a T-shirt that you think brings you luck. Or if you're feeling happy, you choose a bright color that reflects your good mood.

Logic and emotions are always interacting. For example, fear, rage, and joy are triggered by what we observe with our senses. We see something dangerous, and our logical response is to feel fear. On the other hand, emotions can cloud what we think we're seeing. If we're in a fearful mood—for example, if we're out alone at night—even an innocent person can seem threatening.

If you're feeling nervous, you may act in ways that provide you with a feeling of safety, even if those actions aren't logical.

Think Before You Act

Emotions can have an even greater impact on us that we realize. They can actually change the way we think. The physical and chemical effects of emotions can change the focus of our attention. They can affect what we think is most important.

Think about it. Have you ever been angry and texted a message that you later wished you hadn't sent? Your emotions clouded your logic. That's one of the reasons it's never a good idea to make an important decision when you're in an extremely stressful or emotional situation.

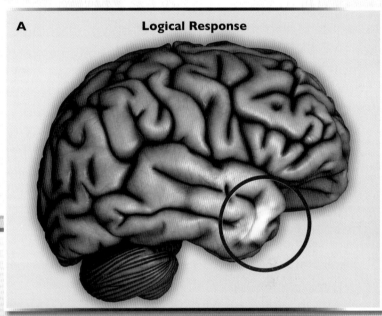

A — Logical Response

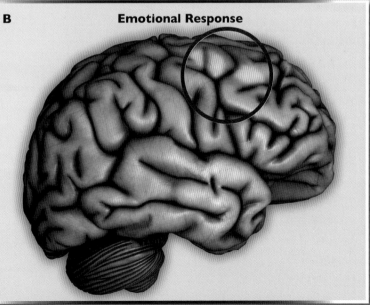

B — Emotional Response

INSIDE KNOWLEDGE

Neuroimaging

Scientists often use a technique called neuroimaging to see what parts of the brain are at work when someone is thinking, or when he or she is feeling a particular emotion. Sections of the brain will literally light up when they are in use. The circled portion of the brain in this photo shows the difference between a logical response (image A) and an emotional response (image B) when a person is confronted with a choice. So when people make a bad decision and later wonder, "What was I thinking?" the answer may be that they were actually feeling.

Feelings Are Important, Too

Emotions can influence our thinking in important ways. Would you want someone making a decision about your health care if that person were only considering costs and time factors? Probably not. You would want at least part of the decision to be based on emotion!

Outside factors can have an effect on whether logic or emotion takes over. For example, researchers have studied something called the "framing effect." They've proved that people will react to a question differently depending on how it is asked. For example, in one experiment, people were shown a film of a car accident. Some were asked how fast the cars were going when they made contact. Others were asked how fast the cars were going when they smashed into each other. The word "smashed" created an emotional reaction. The speed estimates went up about 30 percent.

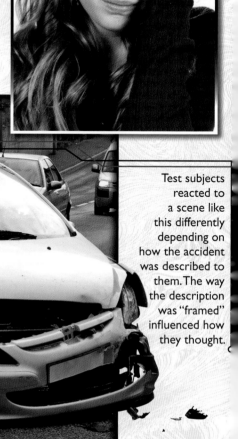

Test subjects reacted to a scene like this differently depending on how the accident was described to them. The way the description was "framed" influenced how they thought.

The bottom line is, both emotions and logic are necessary in decision-making. A few years ago, one scientist studied people who had injured the part of the brain where emotions are generated. Although they seemed to act normally, those in the study lost all ability to experience emotions. As a result, they found it difficult to make decisions although they could logically describe what they should be doing.

Emotions in Real Life: Mass Hysteria

On October 30, 1938, Mercury Theatre On the Air broadcast "War of the Worlds." This was a realistic radio play about a Martian invasion. People tuning in late thought the broadcast was real and began to panic. The panic spread until thousands of people were sure the country was being invaded by creatures from outer space. They said they saw flashes of light in the sky and could smell poison gas.

These listeners were experiencing something called mass hysteria. Mass hysteria is when a group of people with something in common begin to act or think the same way. Because the emotions involved are so strong, mass hysteria can lead to illness, panics, and even to riots.

Many listeners who heard the "War of the Worlds" broadcast believed Earth had been invaded by Martians.

The eyes are black and gleam like a serpent's. The mouth is "V-shaped" with saliva dripping from its rimless lips ...

WHAT SHAPES EMOTIONS?

During a thunderstorm, you dive under a blanket. Your friend stands by the window and waits eagerly for the lightning. If emotions work the same way for all of us, why the difference?

If you ask scientists why humans react differently to the same situations, many will talk about a concept called nature versus nurture. Nature refers to **heredity**—the characteristics we get from our parents. Nurture refers to environment, or our experiences. Even experts are still not sure which influences us more.

Nature

Emotions

Abilities

Health and physical strength

Nurture

Family environment and upbringing

Friends and social situations

Outside events and experiences

They do know that genes play an important role in our emotions and behavior. Genes are inherited characteristics, such as eye and hair color. Genes influence the kinds of emotions and behaviors we will experience. For example, researchers have found a gene associated with anger. A slight chemical difference in that gene determines whether a person is more likely to have angry outbursts or behave violently.

While our genes may give us certain traits and behaviors, our environment decides how we respond to our emotions. How we are raised, where we live, and who our friends are can alter our personalities, emotions, and behaviors.

Friends and Family

Perhaps no one aspect of life influences your emotions more than the people you spend the most time with—your friends and family. That's not surprising. Some of the most emotional events in our lives—births, love, illness, and the death of loved ones—occur in families and among close friends.

Friends can be as important to our emotional health as family members.

Each family member influences the others. If you come from a family that creates an environment of love and respect, chances are you experience mainly positive emotions. But in **dysfunctional** families, there is often conflict, misbehavior, and even abuse. Members of this kind of family feel mostly negative emotions.

Your friends, teachers, and other people you spend time with are, in a way, an extended family. For example, teammates spend a lot of time together. They form strong emotional bonds. Praise from a coach or other players can make an individual feel good. Constant criticism can make that same player feel worthless.

In dysfunctional families, children often fall into various "roles." These roles include
- scapegoat: the child whom parents blame for their problems.
- quiet child: often, the child who is ignored.
- good child: the child who is the family overachiever.
- mascot: the funny child who distracts others from family problems.

When a child plays a role for too long, his or her emotional health is affected. The scapegoat may feel like a bad person. The good child may feel so driven to succeed that he or she never relaxes or has fun.

Sports teams and clubs can build or destroy a person's confidence.

Culture and Emotions

Everyone in the world feels emotions. But emotions can be affected by culture—the country or social group that you are a part of. Generally, there are three things in a culture that affect how we feel and show our emotions:

- **Ideas about which emotions are good and bad**. In the United States, children are encouraged to take pride in their accomplishments. In India, children may heel happier when they have been obidient or helpful.
- **Rules about feeling**. What's the appropriate reaction to a situation? For example, if you're criticized, is the appropriate reaction embarrassment, shame, or anger?
- **Rules about showing emotions**. If you're insulted, is it correct to become angry or to stay calm? Even within the same country, the rules would differ among different groups of people.

These cultural differences can affect not only how a person feels, but also how he or she reacts later. In one culture, an athlete who loses an event might feel shame and withdraw from his team. In another culture, the reaction to shame might be a desire to work even harder and excel the next time he or she plays.

Many cultural differences disappear when people live in the same country for an extended period of time.

OUTSIDE INFLUENCES

What's your favorite color? What's your favorite season? Your answers may have to do with how they make you feel.

The Color of Emotions

Have you ever been "green with envy"? Do you often feel "blue"? Colors don't just describe our emotions. They actually cause emotions. How does that happen?

We see colors because wavelengths of light vary. Our brain is able to tell different colors apart by the **frequency** of the reflected light waves. Some researchers believe a particular color's frequency causes us to experience certain emotions. Colors that have a higher frequency, such as red, seem to cause more positive or "high-energy" emotions than colors with a lower frequency, such as black and brown.

Other researchers think colors affect us in certain ways because we connect them with pleasant or unpleasant things. We connect green with nature, for example. So it gives us a positive feeling.

Wavelength of Light in Nanometers

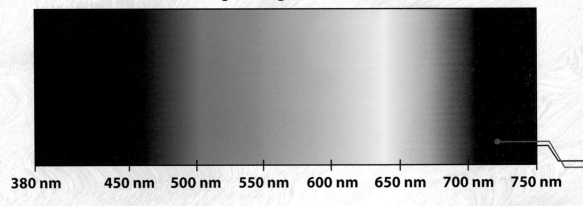

| 380 nm | 450 nm | 500 nm | 550 nm | 600 nm | 650 nm | 700 nm | 750 nm |

The entire range of light wavelengths is called the spectrum. Shorter wavelengths appear as blue and violet, while the longer wavelengths appear red.

Whatever the cause, colors do have an effect on the way we feel. Warm colors, such as red, yellow, and orange, create feelings ranging from warmth and comfort to anger and hostility. Cool colors, such as blue, purple, and green, create feelings of calm. But they may cause feelings of sadness or indifference. Sometimes the emotion created by a color can even change over time. For example, not long ago neon colors were associated with trendy clothes and accessories. They created positive emotions in people. Once those colors became dated, however, they could create feelings of distaste or discomfort.

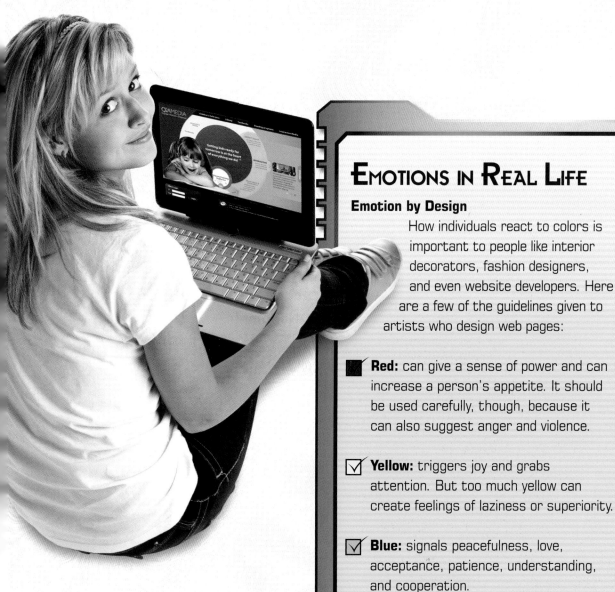

EMOTIONS IN REAL LIFE

Emotion by Design

How individuals react to colors is important to people like interior decorators, fashion designers, and even website developers. Here are a few of the guidelines given to artists who design web pages:

Red: can give a sense of power and can increase a person's appetite. It should be used carefully, though, because it can also suggest anger and violence.

Yellow: triggers joy and grabs attention. But too much yellow can create feelings of laziness or superiority.

Blue: signals peacefulness, love, acceptance, patience, understanding, and cooperation.

The Winter Blues

Weather can cause emotional distress for many people, especially during the winter. Some become "moody," or feel "blue." Others are anxious, or they feel hopeless. They might not go out of the house. They might oversleep and overeat. They are less active.

People who go through these emotional ups and downs might be suffering from seasonal affective disorder (SAD). SAD is a type of depression that occurs around the same time each year. Most people suffer SAD during the winter. Others are miserable during the spring and summer. People who work long hours inside office buildings with few windows may experience symptoms all year.

For some, SAD is only a mildly troublesome disorder. But other people may experience severe depression. When that happens, it's important to seek help.

Even a long stretch of cloudy weather can trigger seasonal affective disorder (SAD).

EMOTIONS IN REAL LIFE

Why so SAD?

Doctors do not yet know the specific causes for SAD. Staff at the Mayo Clinic, a famous medical research and treatment center, list these possibilities:

- **Our "biological clock" (circadian rhythm).** Fewer hours of sunlight in fall and winter may throw off our internal clock. Our body doesn't know if it should sleep or be awake. We become irritable or sad.
- **Melatonin levels.** The change in season can also change the balance of the natural hormone melatonin, which plays a role in sleep patterns and mood.
- **Serotonin levels.** A drop in serotonin, the feel-good neurotransmitter, might play a role in seasonal affective disorder. Reduced sunlight can cause a drop in serotonin. This can lead to feelings of sadness or depression.

People who suffer from SAD are often told to try light therapy, or phototherapy. The patient sits or works near a light therapy box that gives off light similar to natural sunlight. The body is fooled into creating the chemicals and hormones it needs.

It's not just the amount of daylight that can affect emotions, though. Holidays can trigger emotional memories. Being trapped inside during long spells of cold weather can give people "cabin fever." Of course, ongoing rain or fog can also dampen the spirit!

A day or two of sunshine in the middle of winter can dramatically improve a person's mood.

EXTREME EMOTIONS

Everyone gets angry and sad. Most people are able to handle these emotions. Others find them spinning out of control.

Beyond Sadness

Depression is one of the most familiar "extreme emotions." In fact, it is one of the most common health problems in the world. Simply put, depression is a sadness that doesn't go away. But depression isn't simple at all. It's a medical illness that affects the mind and the body.

People suffering from depression have definite symptoms. These symptoms can vary with a person's age or gender. But they often include feelings of hopelessness, problems sleeping, and crying spells that happen for no reason. Depressed people also have trouble making decisions or concentrating on a task. They often feel worthless.

Depression is more than just sadness. It's a severe condition that doesn't go away easily.

What causes depression? Researchers think it's a combination of things. Neuroimaging—pictures of the brain—has shown that physical changes in the brain might be linked to depression. Or, the neurotransmitters in the brain might not be there in the right balance. Genetics may also be a cause. Depression is more common if family members have also suffered from it. Of course, terrible situations can cause depression. The loss of a loved one, a natural disaster, and high stress can all lead to illness.

Interestingly, some people suffer the opposite problem. People in a manic state feel extreme excitement and energy. They may think they can do anything. This may sound good, but it often causes poor judgment and leads to bad choices.

The Ten Symptoms of Clinical Depression

- [ ] A sad, anxious, or "empty" mood that doesn't go away
- [ ] Sleeping too little or sleeping too much
- [ ] Reduced appetite and weight loss or increased appetite and weight gain
- [ ] Loss of interest or pleasure in activities once enjoyed
- [ ] Restlessness or irritability
- [ ] Physical symptoms that don't respond to treatment
- [ ] Difficulty concentrating, remembering, or making decisions
- [ ] Fatigue or loss of energy
- [ ] Feeling guilty, hopeless or worthless
- [ ] Thoughts of death or suicide

A person should seek help if five or more of these symptoms continue for more than two weeks, or if they interfere with daily life.

High Anxiety

Do you ever get anxious before a big test? Perhaps you feel anxious walking alone at night? Anxiety is a useful emotion. It helps us recognize and cope with stressful or dangerous situations. Anxiety is a normal reaction to **stress**.

Sometimes, though, anxiety can get the better of us. Then it is called an anxiety disorder, which means it interferes with how we think or function. Those suffering from extreme anxiety find it hard to lead a normal life. Anxiety disorders affect forty million adults in the United States age eighteen and older.

Anxiety in some situations is normal. But people with an anxiety disorder are in a constant state of tension.

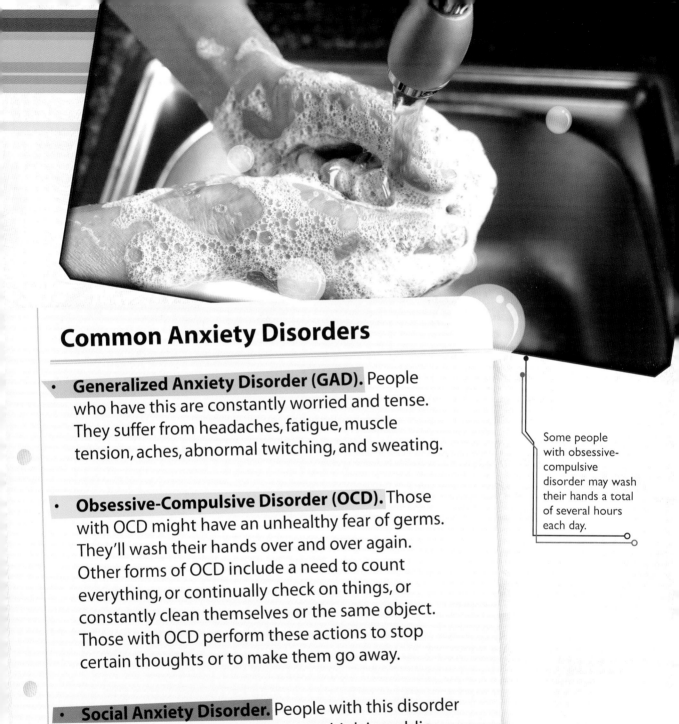

Common Anxiety Disorders

- **Generalized Anxiety Disorder (GAD).** People who have this are constantly worried and tense. They suffer from headaches, fatigue, muscle tension, aches, abnormal twitching, and sweating.

- **Obsessive-Compulsive Disorder (OCD).** Those with OCD might have an unhealthy fear of germs. They'll wash their hands over and over again. Other forms of OCD include a need to count everything, or continually check on things, or constantly clean themselves or the same object. Those with OCD perform these actions to stop certain thoughts or to make them go away.

- **Social Anxiety Disorder.** People with this disorder may not be able to speak, eat, or drink in public. They are afraid of being watched and judged by others. Social anxiety disorder often interferes with school and work and other activities.

Some people with obsessive-compulsive disorder may wash their hands a total of several hours each day.

nxiety disorders can be as harmful to a person as a physical illness. Luckily, these isorders can often be controlled with medication or **therapy**. After treatment, eople can sometimes return to productive, happy lives within a matter of weeks.

People with
agoraphobia may
be afraid to leave
their homes.

A World of Fear

One particular type of anxiety disorder is a phobia. A phobia is a fear that
has gotten out of control. One person may be so terrified of snakes that she
cannot even handle a toy snake. Another may be so afraid of the outside
world that he never leaves the house. Phobias seem to be connected to the
amygdala—the part of the brain that controls fear and aggression.

Phobias, like other anxiety disorders, can lead to panic attacks. The sufferer
may experience
- panic and fear
- rapid heartbeat
- shortness of breath
- trembling
- a strong desire to get away. Scientists think panic attacks are part
  of the fight-or-flight response. The brain is saying, "Run away!"

A study by the National Institute of Mental Health (NIMH) found that up to 8.7 percent of Americans over age eighteen may suffer from phobias. Here are some of the most common.

Agoraphobia: fear of open places

Claustrophobia: fear of tight or closed places

Acrophobia: fear of heights

Mysophobia: fear of germs

Xenophobia: fear of strangers

Necrophobia: fear of dead things

Brontophobia: fear of thunder and lightning

Carcinophobia: fear of cancer

Aviophobia: fear of flying

Arachnophobia: fear of spiders

Some people with phobias go through a treatment called desensitization. They face their fears bit by bit. A person with arachnophobia might first look at the word "spider." Then he or she might look at pictures of spiders, and then films. The process continues until the person can see a real spider and not be terrified.

Remember, though, that some amount of fear in these areas is normal and healthy. They're only phobias if they stop you from living your life.

Managing Emotions

How we deal with emotions, especially negative emotions, is important to our health. Unchecked emotions can cause us to act out in unhealthy ways or make us ill.

Unfortunately, we cannot turn our emotions off like a light. We have to find a way to deal with them. There are two general ways of doing that: through counseling or therapy, and through medication.

Getting Help

Psychologists and **psychotherapists** help people face, accept, and work through their emotions. In regular sessions, therapists help clients explore such questions as "What am I feeling?" and "Why am I feeling this way?" Once people become aware of why they are feeling a certain way, they are better able to control their emotions.

Psychotherapists may also teach people various skills to cope with their emotions. They may suggest such therapies as

- art therapy, which helps people express feelings, emotions, and thoughts through drawing, writing, painting, or music;
- behavior therapy, which changes a person's unhealthy behavior by using a system of rewards;
- cognitive therapy, which changes the thinking patterns that lead to unhealthy feelings and behavior.

Marvelous Medications

Sometimes, emotions may not be primarily caused by outside influences. They may be the result of chemical imbalances or other problems in the brain. In these cases, doctors may prescribe special drugs. These drugs can help adjust the chemical imbalance or change the way the brain is working. People who are depressed might take an antidepressant. Those who suffer severe emotional problems might be given stronger drugs. These treatments are often combined with therapy and can help a person return to a much happier way of life.

Staying in Charge

Emotions are fascinating. They are also a bit of a mystery. But your emotions are yours and no one else's. How you deal with the emotional ups and downs of life is a lot like riding "The Incredible Hulk" at Universal Studios. It's a little scary, but always exciting!

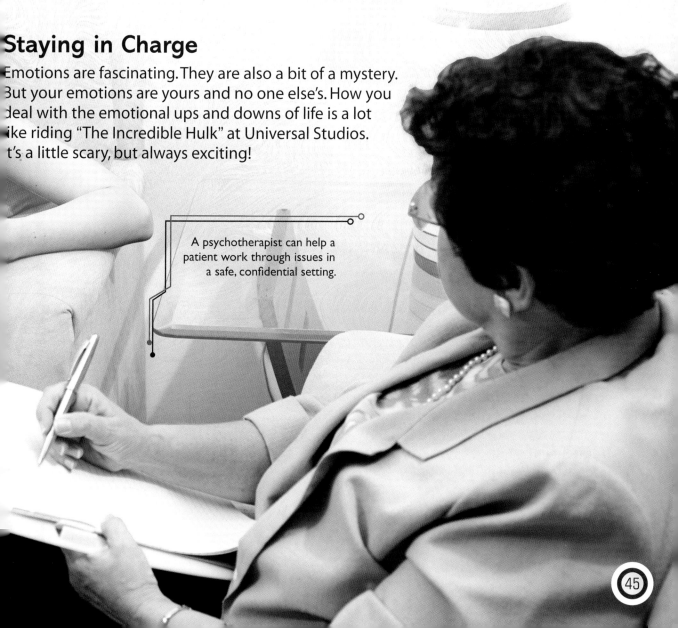

A psychotherapist can help a patient work through issues in a safe, confidential setting.

GLOSSARY

anxiety An unpleasant emotion that arises when danger is imagined but cannot be clearly identified.

anxiety disorder A condition caused by extreme tension.

behavior The manner in which one acts.

biochemical Having to do with the chemistry of living organisms.

body language The gestures, postures, and facial expressions by which a person communicates with others.

carbohydrates A food group that consists of sugars and starches that provide the body with fuel.

cortex The outer layer of the brain.

depression An emotional state characterized by extreme unhappiness that doesn't go away.

dopamine A neurotransmitter that is essential for a healthy nervous system.

dysfunctional The abnormal functioning of a social group, such as a family.

emotional intelligence The way humans respond to the emotions of others.

frequency The rate at which something is repeated over a period of time.

heredity The transmission of traits from parents to their children.

hormones Secretions that enable the body to function.

hypothalamus The part of the brain that relays sensory information to the cerebral cortex.

limbic system The group of interconnected brain cells involved in emotion and behavior.

nerves A bundle of fibers that use chemical and electrical signals to transmit information from one part of the body to the other.

neurological Relating to the brain.

neurotransmitters Chemicals that send signals between nerve cells.

optimistic Hopeful and confident.

physiological Relating to the way an organism functions.

psychotherapist Mental health professional who treats those suffering from emotional, behavioral, and mental disorders.

respiration The process by which the body exchanges oxygen for carbon dioxide.

stress Any event that makes heightened demands on a person's emotional resources.

tertiary Third in order or level.

therapy Treatment meant to relieve a disorder.

Find Out More

Books

Evans-Martin, F. Fay (Editor). *Emotion and Stress*. New York: Chelsea House Publications, 2007. An in-depth explanation of emotions and stress. This book explains how stressful situations generate negative emotions. It also details how emotions and stress impact health.

Crist, James J. *What to Do When You're Scared and Worried: A Guide for Kids*. Minneapolis, MN: Free Spirit Publishing, 2004. This easy-to-follow book is written for kids who struggle with their fears and worries.

Websites

http://library.thinkquest.org/25500/index2.htm
This site gives a short and thoughtful explanation of emotions and behavior. Not only does it detail the various theories on emotions, but it also looks at the effects of emotions.

http://pbskids.org/itsmylife/emotions/index.html
This website from PBS has a special section on kids and their emotions. "My Life" deals with everyday problems that kids face.

INDEX